MEDITATION STORIES
FOR KIDS

Incredibles Tales with Unicorns, Dinosaurs and Dragons

WALT PIXAR

Table of Contents

INTRODUCTION

This book discusses the power of bedtime stories, from how they serve to unleash a child's imagination to how they foster quality time between parents and children, thus leading to healthy physical and psychological development. It also addresses certain techniques within the practices of meditation and mindfulness that can be used with children in order to help them discover mindfulness and calm. Finally, there are a handful of stories included that will encourage adults to make this practice a nightly habit, in the service of peaceful well-being. Let your imagination soar!

Some of the most magical words that a child can hear, especially in those early years, are, "Once upon a time." Those words immediately mark the beginning of something familiar and new; they mark a time that is meant for stopping and listening instead of running to play. They mark a time for settling down. And for many children, they mark the beginning of bedtime and the bedtime routine. These words start many different bedtime stories. They mark the beginnings of adventures and fantasies. They mark the beginnings of fairy tales and mysteries. They are very exciting words; they are full of potential and they tell the child everything without saying anything at all.

CHAPTER 1: GOODBYE TODAY,
HELLO DREAMS!

Introduction for Parents

One of the most difficult daily tasks all of us undertake—
especially those of us who might suffer from insomnia—is the
letting go of all of the events and activities of the day. Many
of us spend sleepless hours turning over and over in our
heads the conversations we had, the argument we had, the
many things that we didn't quite get to but worry about. This
is especially difficult for children who may not be able to
voice their anxieties and fears as eloquently as they would
like. Oftentimes, we are told just to let go and not think about
these things, but this advice is virtually worthless: if we could

just relax, stop thinking, and sleep, we just simply would. Instead, taking a meditative journey through this tangle of thoughts can help us find peace with them. We don't necessarily get rid of thoughts, but we can learn how to unfurl them, to reframe them so that we can sleep in peace. This can help a child let go of the events of the day in order to soothe them into a restful sleep.

This kind of restful sleep is dependent on getting deep sleep: getting to the REM stage of sleep is crucial to getting the kind of rest that recharges you and energizes you for the next day. What many of us do not know is that we have a degree of control over our dreams, as well as the fact that dreams help us access a state of restfulness. The concept of lucid dreaming describes a kind of meditative state where we can access the most creative and open parts of our mind; regular dreaming is when we achieve deep, healing sleep. Guiding your children into dreams is a meditative practice that they can use to bolster their imaginations and achieve truly restful sleep. The following meditation helps children release the stress of the day and swim gently into the dream world.

Meditation for Children

Let's start to think about everything that happened today, while we start to use our breath. Breathe in and out, in and out, slowly and steadily, as you just think about what happened today. Start with the morning and remember how you felt when you woke up. Think about what happened after breakfast and at school. Remember what you did and said, just calmly thinking about everything that went on today, while you breathe in and out, slowly. This is just a quick review of your day, whatever happened, and it doesn't matter if it was good or bad, just that it was. Keep your breathing steady as you go through all these thoughts in your mind.

Let yourself know: everything that I am thinking is okay. This is not about telling yourself what to think about things; it is just about understanding that what happened did happen. You are okay with it. And, now, tomorrow will be a different day. There is no need to stay stuck in everything that happened today. You are letting yourself see it, remember it, and this is giving yourself permission to feel exactly what you feel. Everyone has feelings, some that are good and some that are bad: your feelings are just what they are, and nobody can tell you how to feel about them. It's okay if sometimes things bother you. Trying to pretend like they don't just keeps you stuck in sadness or anger. What you can do is to breathe through all these thoughts and understand that whatever happened today already happened. It's gone, and tomorrow will be another day. You are in the present, in the here and now, breathing through your thoughts, each in turn. Breathe in and nod your head: yes, that happened. Then breathe out, and let it go. Take a few moments to think about all the little things that happened during the day, then start releasing them all, as if they were balloons filled with helium floating gently away from your mind. Breathe in, see a balloon. Breathe out, let it float away.

As you watch these balloons float gently away, imagine that you are just yourself, the best person you can be. You are not what happened today; you are not what other people think. You are not, even, your thoughts; you are a great deal more than that, and you are free to let go of all these thoughts each day as you travel gently into sleep and into the next day. Moment by moment, you are still just yourself, happy and calm and loved. You are even showing yourself love by letting the past float away from, leaving yourself happy and peaceful. You are all that you need, right now, perfectly as you are. And everything is perfect as it is. You are just as perfect as you are. Breathe for a few minutes, experiencing how light you feel as these thought balloons float away from you.

Now notice your body again. Check in with each part of your body, just as you checked in with all your thoughts, and follow the natural rhythms of your breathing to let your body relax and go loose. Start with the bottoms of your feet, your toes, your ankles, checking in with each in its turn, and simply thanking them for being there. From your feet, move on to your shins and thighs, noticing how everything feels, and saying thank you for helping me get through each day. Inhale into your lungs and belly, and as you let your breath out, let your body go limp. Breathe into and relax your throat, your jaw and face, and let your shoulders ease down, your arms relaxed by your side. Allow your head to relax, feeling the top of your head almost float, because it feels so light from letting go of everything that happened. You are just still and calm, present, and serene. Breathe into your body for a few moments.

Now imagine that your mind is a blank slate: take each thought that exists, every memory of the daily activity, every event that you are still thinking about, and continue to send them away as little floating balloons. These thoughts will come back to you, but you don't need them right now: you are clearing your mind of clutter. Keep your breath calm and steady, inhaling, and exhaling with the rhythms of your body, letting those thoughts float away from you. You are relaxed and clear. Your mind is floating and free.

Now picture yourself on an island: you are on a tiny speck of land in the middle of a vast ocean; you can hear the slow rhythmic sloshing of the surf against the land; you can feel the spray of ocean water on your face; you can taste the salt in the air. The sun is distant and mild; it is warm and comfortable. You are on an island, and there is nothing else on this island but you, and this island is in the middle of a vast ocean. You can see no other shorelines, no other people. You are at peace and comfy on your island. This is your imagination working, and you can make your island exactly what you wish it to be. Start to notice the island underneath you, this island that you have dreamed up in your mind. You can literally feel the ground moving beneath you, being gently rocked by the movements of the ocean. Your body and mind feel grounded, connected to the island, and yet you are aware of a floating sensation, the feeling that you might be floating away, just like your thoughts. Your island is a safe haven in the middle of the vast ocean, and you can feel our body almost floating above it. Keep your breath slow and steady, inhaling and exhaling as the waves come rolling slowly in and out, in and out. Your body is light, and your mind is clear.

Imagine that your mind and body start to become free of the earth; this island that you dreamed up is a place to go when you want to float away from it all. You are opening yourself up to a whole universe of thoughts, ideas, and energy. You can feel your mind, even your body, floating free of the island. You are rising up to a higher plane, and you can feel your mind looking up into the big sky and out into the great universe. As you allow yourself to rise, up and up and away, you can see the speck of the island below you, waiting for your safe return, as you allow yourself to go up into the sky. You are not flying, but you are floating, allowing your mind to imagine its way up into the atmosphere. What do you see? What do you feel? Take a moment with your breath to let your mind soar.

Now imagine that you slip the bounds of earth entirely, your mind and even your body floating ever further upward until you begin to reach the velvety blackness of space. There are stars far away around you, planets, and galaxies, and you are a mindful entity accessing these celestial bodies, feeling their rhythms within you just as your breathing is in tune with this cosmic dance. Let your mind roam these corners of the universe, noticing the stars and planets and asteroids and comets, being so happy in your imagined world. You are breathing and feeling and welcoming the wonderful patterns of the universe. Let your mind roam, and allow it to dream up what it will.

Perhaps you see a distant star, giant and red, glowing with energy and expelling its matter out into the universe. You are swimming in its energy, connecting with its deepest understandings of the vastness of the universe, of the importance of your dreaming mind within it. This star is giving out its life so that you can have yours; you are an awesome part of this big universe, and your floating, open mind welcomes all it has to offer. You are swimming through the dust and stuff of this giant, red star, allowing your mind to dream along with it. Breathe in this stardust, allow it to take your mind where it will. Breathe in with happiness and joy; breathe out with calmness and peace. You are becoming a part of the universal magic; your mind is open to new, all new things and new beginnings.

Perhaps you encounter a comet, traveling from one world to the next, a ball of mineral and ice made pure energy, trailing stardust in its wake. You join this comet on its journey, streaking through the vast blackness of space; your mind and body are as free as the weightlessness of that space around you. You notice the universal dance performing around you as you shoot from planet to planet, seeing galaxies vast as whole continents out of the corner of your eye. Your mind is on a cosmic journey, and let it notice what it notices. Let your mind peek into the corners of space, open to whatever comes its way. The comet is taking you on a universal journey. Take some moments here just to enjoy the ride, breathing in harmony.

When you are ready, let the comet bring you back to earth, to your little island, which you see as a speck in the distance, growing closer and bluer with each moment. You tumble through the atmosphere, feeling your weight come back to you, your body warming with the sunlight. You can eventually see the tiny dot that is your island, calm and serene, awaiting your return. You can see your physical self still sitting or lying down on the island, breathing and relaxed. You have dreamed your way out into the vastness of space and back. Now you are ready to dream many, many fabulous dreams, resting your mind for your earthly journey of tomorrow.

CHAPTER 2: BASIC BEDTIME STORIES: FROM THE MOUNTAINS TO THE SEAS

As we leave behind the seasons, there is another very important aspect to consider for any bedtime story—the environments of the world. Your child is likely used to just the climate in your own area. If you live somewhere coastal, all your child will know is coastal weather and environments unless you travel. If you live in the middle of the plains, your child is used to a flat world with an ever-expanding sky on the horizon. This is not a problem—but it does lead to children wondering about what it would be like to go very far away. Children who live in a rainy area, like Seattle, may fantasize about going to a hot, sandy desert. Children who live in the mountains may wonder what it would be like to see the sea, far and ever expanding.

This is only natural—our environments shape us and they are all very different. There are environments that are great and flat. There are environments that are so densely full of trees that you cannot see the sky! There are areas where you are surrounded by endless ocean, especially in islands. The world, and the lands within it, are widely different, and those differences should be celebrated. Your child should be encouraged to learn about these different *biomes*—areas in the world that are greatly different from one another.

We learn about biomes in school; they are usually taught as a part of science class, along with the diversity of animal and plant life, as well as the different ways in which you can explore the world. We have seven major biomes in our wonderful diverse earth. Each of these have their own unique features to offer. Each of them are known for their own different animal species and environments. There are tropical rainforests, known for their constant rain. They are usually filled up with tropical plants and wildlife. They are full of water and growth, and there are few areas in the world that can rival the sheer diversity of species within these environments.

There are temperate forests—areas that are forested but still have their own four seasons. These forests may consist of leafy trees, or they may be evergreen, but the seasons still pass from spring to summer to autumn and then winter. They are full of all sorts of well-known wildlife; bears and wolves love these forests, as well as squirrels and deer.

There are boreal forests—these are mostly just evergreen trees; primarily the conifers and they are very old and very mysterious. These forests are green all year round, and they have very long and cold winters.

Then, there are lands that are not full of trees at all—deserts are largely barren. They have some plants, but they are sparse, and those that exist are designed to be harsh and unwilling to give out their precious liquids that they hold within themselves. Think of the cacti and their spines, designed so that animals cannot easily steal their liquid. These deserts are full of heat all summer, but they are also cold in the winter.

There are grasslands as well—hills and flat lands that are full of nothing but grass and without any trees at all. They are rainy enough for plants to grow, but when it comes to summers, fires usually ravage them, destroying the chance for trees. Savannas are much like grasslands, but they also have some trees as well. And finally, tundra are large and flat with low grass as well. But, the tundra is cold. It is very bitterly cold and many of them are frozen.

From mountains to seas, you can explore many of these wonderfully unique biomes. You can meet animals that want to play out and about. You can see landscapes so unique that you never would have thought possible. You can see oceans lapping against sand dunes, or you can see great, frozen plains.

You do not even have to step outside of your home to explore these widely expansive lands, either—you can explore them from the safety and comfort of your home. You can read about them in books. You can meet the animals in them. You can explore the beauty of them without much effort at all.

In the next stories, your child is going to explore through several different biomes—they are going to explore a boreal forest. They will discover a desert and the widely diverse life that can be found, even when at a glance, it appears to be lifeless. They will discover life on the tundra, exploring the world. They will meet animals that live high up in the mountains, and finally, they will explore a tropical island, far out in the middle of the ocean.

Exploration and curiosity are fundamental parts of childhood; they are endlessly fascinating and wonderfully compelling, and through books, we can explore them. We can learn about the world without feeling like we are learning, all by making it enjoyable, and these stories will, hopefully, do just that. Your child will get to explore the world as he or she reads, and that can be great fun for anyone.

CHAPTER 3: AURORA FOREST

Once upon a time, there lived a pair of twins. There was Arthur, who would proudly tell anyone that would listen that he was the older brother. And, there was Alia, who would usually groan and roll her eyes, whispering loudly to the other person that he was only older by *two minutes*. They both loved each other greatly, and they shared a very important secret with each other. No one else could know their very important secret, and it is so secret, in fact, that even you must remember not to tell anyone else about it when you are let in on what it is.

Their very important secret is that both of them have a very special power; they can talk to animals. For as long as they have both lived, they were able to talk to animals around them. When they had told their parents when they were younger, they got quick pats on the heads and quiet, "That's nice, dear!" in response, and so, from then on, they kept it very secret.

But, that wasn't the only thing that made Arthur and Alia very special. In fact, Arthur and Alia also got to travel the world! You see, their parents were very important people—they were diplomats. That was a very special way of saying that they were responsible for traveling the world to talk to people far and wide. They would go to many, many different countries, and their parents would oftentimes be very busy while they were there. This, of course, left Arthur and Alia with plenty of time to explore all around them when they finished their schoolwork! They were both homeschooled because they traveled so often, but they were always very quick to get all of their work done so they would be able to keep exploring. When they asked to do something, they were always told that they could go, as long as they were very careful to stay close to their home and so long as they were always very careful not to talk to strangers.

Of course, their parents never said that they could not talk to animals.

One day, Arthur and Alia were staying deep in northern Canada. They were so far north that it was dark almost all of the time! It was late in the winter, and the sun was set to be down for a long, long time. It was so strange to see that it was so dark, even during the day! But, Arthur and Alia were not afraid; they were no strangers to exploring in strange, new places, and they welcomed the change! So, after they finished their school, they asked if they could go outside for a little bit.

Their parents looked surprised—it was very snowy outside and it was very cold, and there was no sun anywhere! But, when the children gave their best puppy dog eyes, begging and saying, "Please!" as loudly as they could, Arthur and Alia's parents sighed and nodded.

"Fine!" said their mother. "But, you must stay right in the front area!" They were staying in a hotel in a very small village that was on the outskirts of a great, big forest. The forest, though it was dark and hard to see, had great, big, tall conifer trees—the trees that are shaped like cones. The trees were tall and skinny and looked very different from the big, bushy, fat pine trees that Alia and Arthur were used to seeing.

Happily, both children rushed to put on as much of their winter gear as they could—it was so cold that they needed it all! They had their thermal underwear, and then a layer of clothes. They had socks, and then wool socks. They had a fleece jacket, and then thick snow pants. They had great, big parkas and they had fuzzy hats. They had gloves to cover their hands and masks and goggles to protect their faces. Finally, they had boots that went over their feet.

"I feel like a marshmallow!" puffed Alia as they both made their way outside. Even wearing everything that they had on, it still felt chilly. But, being able to go outside in the middle of the day and have it be pitch black was worth it! They were very excited to see what they could see all around them! So, off they went, waddling through the yard to the hotel. They were wearing so many different layers that they could not walk normally at all! Off they went, slowly ambling around the yard. It was tough work, trudging through all of that snow! But, it was still fun and they were certain that it would be worth it.

Soon, they heard something happening behind them. It was the quiet crunching of snow of little paws. As quickly as they could, which admittedly, was not very quickly at all with all of their winter gear on, they turned around, and standing there, staring at them, was a little white fox. It had golden eyes that gleamed in the light that was coming out from the window, and it was staring at them. But then, it laughed at them. It must have known something that they didn't know.

"What's so funny?" asked Arthur, embarrassed. Although it could not be seen underneath his hat and his mask, he was blushing. No one liked to be laughed at!

But, upon hearing Arthur speak, the fox stopped. It stared at him for a moment. "Why are you talking like I'm talking?" asked the fox. It was very surprised to hear that a human was speaking in a way that it could understand.

"What do you mean why? I just am!" snapped Arthur. "Why are you laughing at us!"

"Arthur, shh!" said Alia. She did not want to deal with a fight at all. She simply wanted to get going to explore. "Arthur, leave it alone. It's cute!"

The fox stared at Alia, and then back to Arthur. "You both speak," it said flatly. It seemed disappointed somehow, but then, it shook itself off and sat down. Its fur was very fluffy and was almost invisible in the snow. If it weren't for the fox's eyes and nose, Arthur was pretty sure that he would not be able to see it at all.

"We do indeed," said Arthur, scowling at the fox. "Do you have a problem with that?"

"Only if you have a problem with listening," was the fox's simple reply. "But, you should know something—the pack of wolves is coming through here soon! They all go up through the forest and toward the top of the hills so they can howl or something at the aurora when it shines tonight." When the fox mentioned howling, she rolled her eyes, as if she thought the idea was very silly.

"Ooh, there's gonna be an aurora?" squealed Alia. She had always wanted to see one, but when she had asked her mother about it when they were going to their current village, her mother shrugged her shoulders and said that she would see.

"Oh, boy," said Arthur, putting a hand on his head in exasperation. "Here we go."

"Can you take us there? Please? Please? PLEASE?!" Alia was practically bouncing in her boots as she stared down the fox. She was very excited about the idea of potentially going to go and see something wonderful like that. It was like a once in a lifetime possibility for her! And, even better, there would be a pack of wolves there! It would be great!

The fox looked at her like she had grown another head. "Why?"

"Because it's wonderful and beautiful and I've always wanted to go and see it!" She crossed her arms firmly in front of her. "Do you have a problem with that?" Alia was very determined to go and see such a wonderful sight. She had seen pictures, and it had always looked like the sky was on fire.

The fox shook her head. "No way am I going. I avoid those wolves as much as I can. They're a bunch of stinky followers. I prefer to spend my time by myself, thank you!"

Alia's face fell behind her winter gear.

"But!" said the fox, as if sensing her disappointment, "You can get there yourself. All you have to do is wait for the wolves to pass and then follow their footsteps. They're usually so busy howling," and she rolled her eyes again in disapproval,

31

"That they never notice anything at all. Why, I bet that I could steal one of their silly chewing bones that they like to carry around and they'd never notice!"

Alia grinned. She turned to look at Arthur, and all he could see where her shining eyes, staring up at him pleadingly. They were full of longing and excitement, and Arthur sighed. He could not resist. "Fine!" he said, "But only because you're my little sister!"

Alia didn't even fight it that time. She flung her arms around Arthur's neck and squeezed him tightly. "Thanks! You're the best brother ever!"

"I'm your only brother!" he snapped back.

"That means less competition!" replied Alia.

"Well, I'm out of here!" said the fox. "Good luck with your howling at the aurora." And off went the fox. She seemed to melt away into the snow, disappearing.

Then, they saw them. The wolves were coming. First, it was just one, walking along near them. It was massive! It was easily bigger than any dog they had ever seen, and it walked right past them. As soon as the first one appeared, many more started to appear as well. They were like ghosts, slowly materializing in front of them out of nowhere, first with their great, big ears, and then with their bodies. Occasionally, one would glance over at the two bundled up children, but they did not seem interested in them at all.

And, just as quickly as the wolves appeared, and just as quietly, too, they all vanished into the gently falling snow, leaving behind nothing but the footprints behind them.

"Woah," whispered Alia, breaking the silence that hung in the air, dampened by the snow that fell.

"Yeah," Arthur whispered back. "Talk about incredible!" And for most children their age, it was! But, that did not deter them at all. "Ready?" asked Arthur. He was starting to feel just as excited to go now, too!

Alia nodded her head, still too stunned by the majestic presence of the wolves as they had silently drifted right past them.

So, off they went, quietly following the path of the wolves. They went through some trees that seemed to be so tall that they reached the sky. Occasionally, they heard the quiet hoot of an owl, but for the most part, the world was silent; it was eerie.

Soon, they heard a howl, and that's when they realized that they had to be getting close. Then, the howling got louder and louder, and when Alia looked up, she could see the appearance of what looked like the occasional flash of green up in the sky, and not much later, they made it all the way to a great, big clearing! The clearing was wide open, overlooking a big cliff, and atop the cliff, they could see the silhouettes of the wolves, sitting there. One by one, they sang their song. Each wolf would let out a single long, sorrowful note. Then, another and another.

Alia looked up and was shocked at what she saw. The sky was dancing! There were great, beautiful blurs of green, waving and undulating across the dark sky. There were other colors mixed in there, too—she could see purples and what almost looked like a teal. They were beautiful and even better than anything she had ever seen before. They were so much better than the ones she had seen in the pictures, and even better— she got to see them with the beautiful, haunting baying of the wolves.

Alia and Arthur stood there, next to each other in silence. They were enthralled with the sights and neither of them could have ever fathomed just how wonderful it would have been. As the wolves began to slow down their songs, Arthur tugged at Alia's hand. "Let's go before they do."

Alia nodded her head, taking one last look at the lights. She had never seen something as wonderful as that, and she highly doubted that she would ever see something as wonderful as that again.

It did not take long for Alia and Arthur to slip back to the hotel, and it looked like their parents had not even noticed that they were missing. But, the same fox was curled up on the step.

"So? Was it worth it?" asked the fox.

"Absolutely," they both replied.

CHAPTER 4: THE SECRET MIRAGE

Once upon a time, there lived a pair of twins. Perhaps you have heard of them—one of them was named Arthur, and he was the bossier of the two. The other was named Alia, and she was very adventurous and fearless. Arthur and Alia were very lucky children, for their parents traveled the world constantly for work, and the twins got to go with them everywhere, too! The twins were always taken where the parents had to go, and that meant that the twins got to go more places a month than many people would go in their entire lifetimes!

Alia and Arthur were special for another reason, however—they had a very secret, very special gift. They were gifted with the ability to talk to animals! So, while their parents were busy in all of these great, new places, Arthur and Alia would spend time in the wilderness. They would speak to animals and learn all sorts of great, new things when they did so. Sometimes, what they learned would be exciting! Sometimes, they learned very important life lessons. Sometimes, they simply learned to appreciate the world around them and everything that they got to do, for they knew that they were very lucky to have the life that they did. They knew that they were very lucky to be able to travel the world and see the great and wondrous sights that they had seen.

One day, their family got on an airplane and flew away to the great new country of Egypt. Alia and Arthur's parents had some very important work to do, and the twins were very excited as well—the new place meant that they would be able to go and explore the desert! They had been to deserts before, but never to one in Egypt. In fact, they had never been to Egypt at all!

"You'll love the pyramids," said their mother as she typed away on her computer. She was a very busy woman with a very important job.

"You'll love the sphinx, too!" said their father, also typing on his computer. He, too, had a very important job. They both worked so they could help other people, and they both did very good jobs of it—they did such good jobs that they were allowed to work together and bring their children everywhere that they went.

The children nodded their heads in agreement, but they knew the truth. Alia wanted to speak to a camel, and Arthur was hoping that they would discover a cobra. Alia, of course, reminded him that snakes rarely liked to talk, and rather, would prefer to bite first and ask questions later, but Arthur still kept his fingers crossed.

They all made it to their hotel in Giza, far in the Egyptian desert, and it was very hot! Alia and Arthur knew that it was going to be hot and dry, but they had no idea just how hot and dry it would be! The sun felt like it was burning on their shoulders and they felt so tired and drained by the warmth of the air. But, it was exciting because they were going on a great adventure! It would be a wondrous thing to go out and explore everything around them. So, like good children, they waited for their parents to get busy with their work, and as soon as they were, off the children went!

They slipped outside and looked around. The sun had set a bit, but it was still hot, even without the sun at its peak. The children were dressed in shorts and tank tops, but still, they felt warm. Their hotel was just outside of the great, big city, and they could see nothing but sand for miles. "Where should we go first?" asked Alia.

Arthur shrugged. He wasn't sure it really mattered when there was nothing to be seen anyway. It was all so flat! They definitely weren't seeing any camels any time soon! But, who knew—they might! "That way, I guess," he added, pointing straight ahead. At least, if they stayed going straight in one direction, it would be harder to get lost.

Alia agreed and off they went. They moved very slowly through the heat. They were not happy at all about it, and they were very glad that they had remembered to wear their sunscreen.

Soon, Alia began to sweat, a lot. She wiped her forehead and sighed. "Are we there yet?" she asked with a groan.

"We can turn around," suggested Arthur, also feeling very warm himself. But, the idea of turning around seemed to perk Alia right back up, and she shook her head. She would rather keep exploring, even if miserably hot. Besides, it was good to get out of the comfort zone, right?

Before long, Arthur stopped. He squinted his eyes tightly and stared at something very far in the distance. "What is that?" he asked his sister, his gaze never moving.

"What's what?" asked Alia, for she did not see a single thing on the horizon. As far as her eyes could see, there was nothing but sand for miles and miles around them. She didn't even see hills! Just golden sands and the blue sky.

"That shape! It looks like... I don't know, an elephant maybe? Do elephants live in Egypt?" He stared harder and harder, but he could not tell what it was in front of him on the horizon. He could not figure out what it was, but that was okay, as he had brought binoculars with him!

Alia shrugged her shoulders. She was unsure whether or not there were any elephants in Egypt, but she did not think so— at least, as far as she knew. "I didn't read about them in my book," she offered, but that was about all of the information she had.

"Well, I see an elephant!" he said as he dug through his backpack to pull out the binoculars. But, as soon as he held them up to his eyes, he frowned. Arthur lowered the binoculars and shook his head and rubbed his eyes. But then, when he looked at the horizon, they were still there. He could still see the elephants!

Alia frowned. "Are you okay?" she asked, her brow furrowing with worry as she reached out to touch Arthur's forehead. "Are you getting heat stroke or something? Maybe you should drink some water like Mom said we should," and she offered him her water bottle.

But, Arthur shook his head firmly. "No!" he replied. "I'm fine! But, I'm seeing something that's there until I use the binoculars."

"That doesn't sound fine to me," added Alia. In fact, that sounded like the opposite of fine—that sounded like hallucinations, and hallucinations were from other problems, such as getting too hot.

"That sounds like a mirage," said a voice behind the twins, and when they turned around, they saw a small, brown weasel with tiny, beady black eyes. It was staring at them both, standing up on two legs. It tilted its little head and watched them both, staring at the water bottle in Alia's hand.

"A mirage?" asked Alia.

The weasel blinked in surprise. Had that human heard it? But, the human had water, so that was enough reason to agree. So, the weasel nodded its head, bobbing up and down. "Yes! A mirage!" he squeaked up. "If you can't see it at any other angle and no one else can see it either, it must be a mirage!"

"What's a mirage?" asked Alia.

Arthur rolled his eyes at his sister's question. The weasel was right—a mirage made perfect sense! "It's when your eyes trick you!" he replied to his sister. "It's when you see something because of the way that the light bends on the sky from the sun. That's why I can see the elephant standing there, but it disappears when I use the binoculars! Hey, thanks, little weasel! You were absolutely right!"

"But," replied the weasel, "What is my reward?" The weasel grinned up at Alia and Arthur, licking his lips and staring at the water.

"Are you thirsty?" asked the twins.

"Oh, yes!" said the weasel. "I'm very thirsty!"

So, the twins gave the weasel some water, and then headed on their way. They were not done exploring yet!

Soon, Alia noticed something dark in the distance, too. "Um, Arthur?" she said uncertainly, "I think I'm seeing a mirage now, too."

"Oh yeah?" he said absently, taking a swig of his own bottle of water before offering it over for Alia to take a drink, too.

"Yeah!" said Alia. "I see a big dark spot on the horizon. It kinda looks like a little black cloud or a big, leafy tree or something.

"Really?" said Arthur, and he turned his attention to the same spot that Alia was pointing. "Well, I see it too!" he told her.

But, neither of them knew what it was, so they both went as quickly as they could to go and see what it could have been. They were both very curious about what was sitting out there for them, but they would have to keep on walking to find out.

Before long, they saw trees! More than one! And, they could see the shimmering of water in the sunlight!

"It's an oasis!" cried Alia, and as soon as they were close enough, she ran as quickly as she could toward it.

"Great!" echoed Arthur, also running as quickly as he could to see what it was. They were very excited to see it up close! An oasis was a wonderful thing to find out in the wild!

As they got closer, they realized that there were several spiky trees nearby. They were not fluffy or leafy at all—rather, they had great, big spiky ferns that stuck out from the top, kind of like a messy feather duster. They all surrounded a great, big pool of water that looked absolutely perfect to go into, and there were great, big patches of grass surrounding it. As they approached, they realized that the oasis was filled up with all sorts of different animals!

There were a few little foxes with ears that were almost comically large—it looked like their ears would make them tip over if they were not careful! They saw a few camels, drinking water from the oasis as well. They were very carefully sipping away at the water there. They saw a few more weasels and mice, too. There were so many different animals, all scattered throughout the desert oasis!

"No wonder we did not see any when we were walking here!" exclaimed Alia, and she was right! It seemed like all of the animals tried to stick to the oasis, and for good reason. Even the air around that great big pool of water felt better! It was cooler and easier to cope with, even though they were still in just as much sun as they were before.

Arthur nodded his head and moved as close to the water as he could without falling in. It was surprisingly deep, and he wondered where all that water came from. It looked like it had been there for quite a while since there were so many big trees surrounding it! But, one thing was very obvious—there were no people here at all!

"I wonder if anyone else has ever been here before!" exclaimed Alia, as if she were reading Arthur's mind.

"I don't know," said Arthur, "But we're the only ones here right now!" He looked over the water again. "Are you thinking what I'm thinking?" asked Arthur, looking at his sister with a mischievous smile.

"Uh oh," she replied, her own grin beginning to stretch across her face. "What is it this time, troublemaker?" she asked him.

"Let's go swimming!" he answered. It was so hot that swimming felt like the only right choice in the first place! If they did not go swimming, he was not sure they would tolerate the heat!

"Okay!" replied Alia with a wide smile, and she sat down her bag and took off her shoes. Then, she ran as quickly as her feet would take her to the water. Her feet sank into the hot sand with each and every step, with the sand getting all between her toes and tickling her, but she didn't mind! She had her eyes on the prize and she was going to get it!

And, with a very quick jump, she landed in the water, laughing and splashing and squealing. The water felt great in the midst of all of the heat that they had dealt with! So, Alia and Arthur spent the rest of their day, splashing and playing in their very special, super-secret oasis. They may not have met a camel or a cobra, but they had gotten to go to some very exciting, very new places and that was good enough for both of them!

CHAPTER 5: TUNDRA TROUBLES

Once upon a time, there lived twins that traveled around the world with their family. Their mother and father were very busy with work, and they would often allow their children to explore as much as they wanted when they went places. The twins were named Arthur, who was exactly two minutes older, thank you very much, and Alia, who hated when her brother rubbed the age difference in her face. Arthur and Alia loved each other greatly, and even though they fought like siblings do, they still always worked very hard to take care of each other.

But, Arthur and Alia were very special children, and not just because they were twins. They were very special for another unique reason—they had a special superpower. They could talk to any animals that they met! And, since they were often all alone and very bored when they traveled, they would go out and make new friends—animals in the area in the world where they traveled. They often traveled somewhere new every few days, usually visiting up to 50 new places each and every year! It was always very exciting to go new places and try new things, and they always worked very hard to be able to make it as easy as possible on their parents. They did not want to make their parents work too hard when they knew that they were already busy, so they kept to themselves and tried their hardest to stay out of trouble as much as they could.

One day, they all hopped on a plane to go to a country called Greenland—Greenland was very far north, and they were going all the way to the northernmost part that time. They were going there so their parents could do some very important work with some very important people to help them. Alia and Arthur did not know exactly what their parents were doing, but they knew that it was very important that they were left alone for the day.

So, when they all got settled in their newest lodging, a tiny inn that overlooked an icy sea, the twins decided that they would poke around outside and see what they could see. The sky was very blue, and very cold, and the ocean looked very dark. The land was flat and not much really seemed to grow there; even though it was summer, the ground was mostly flat, rocky, and it had some reddish and brownish plants growing across it.

"I can see chunks of ice floating out in the ocean!" said Alia, pointing out at an iceberg that was floating by. It didn't look very big, but Alia knew from lots of reading for their schoolwork that icebergs were mostly under the water anyway. Only a very small bit of them floated up on the surface.

"I can see it, too!" said Arthur. They looked at each other and grinned, and then pulled their coats on tighter. Even though it was spring, it was still very chilly for them, especially because they had just spent the week in Egypt, looking at pyramids and exploring in oases while they waited for their parents. They had had a great time, and they had even met some camels on their way to the airport, but, now that they were in Greenland and so far north, it felt even colder than ever!

But, cold or not, they knew that they could never pass up an opportunity for a grand new adventure! So, they looked around. There weren't many buildings, and there really wasn't much at all. It was strangely quiet there, standing and overlooking the sea. All they could hear was the sound of the waves, lapping up at the rocky beach. There were no birds singing. There were no bugs buzzing. There wasn't even the constant drone of traffic nearby. It was entirely silent, aside from those drifting waves, and that was almost unnerving.

Alia looked around once more, and then randomly pointed. She pointed away from the sea. "Let's go that way!" she told her brother, and he simply shrugged his shoulders in response; he didn't care where they went because he didn't really have any plans for the trip that they were on in the first place. Where they went did not matter to him, so long as he got to spend time with his sister and go somewhere new.

So, off they went, in search of anything they could find in they great, wide world around them! Alia was very excited to go exploring everywhere that she could. She skipped ahead of her brother, stopping every now and then to look around. Soon, she stopped entirely and looked down at the ground intently. She was staring at something.

"What are you looking at?" asked Arthur.

"I don't know," said Alia. "Maybe a footprint or something? Who knows what it is!" She pointed at it and scooted over just enough for her brother to take a look too, and he shrugged his shoulders, too.

It looked like a footprint, but it wasn't one that they had ever seen before. And, there was a strange chunk of white fuzz in the middle of it. How weird! "Should we look around to see what made it?" asked Alia.

Arthur looked down at it and shook his head. "Look how big it is—it is bigger than your hand!" he told her, and he was right; the mark on the ground was definitely very big and they had no way to know what had made it. In fact, they had no way to know if whatever had made it in the first place was even safe to be around! He remembered reading in a book on the plane over that there were polar bears in the area. They weren't common and they usually liked to stick to the beach, but they were there sometimes, and polar bears could be very mean!

Arthur shuddered and tightened his coat onto him, trying to push that thought away. What good would it possibly do to think about polar bears being dangerous? What good would it possibly do to scare his sister? So, he remained quiet about the possibility of it being a bear. Besides, what if it was something else all along? He didn't want to overreact.

Soon, Alia stopped again. She was looking down at something else on the ground. Again, there was a great big chunk of white fluff on the ground, this time, stuck between some of the rough shrubs that were there. It looked very warm and very soft. Alia reached out to poke it.

"Don't touch it!" said Arthur.

"Why not?" Alia looked confused.

"Well... You don't know what it is." Arthur realized that he did not really have a good reason to tell Alia no; he just wanted to make sure that she was safe, and the best way to do that felt like it was making sure that she didn't touch anything.

But, Alia would not be deterred! She reached out and petted the fluffy material very quickly with her hand. She squeezed it in her fingers. "Wow! It's really nice to touch!" she told her brother and picked it up. "It feels like fur. Feel it!"

Arthur pulled back and shook his head. He didn't want to! He didn't want to smell like whatever it was that dropped that fluff—he was certain that if he did smell like whatever that was, he would have a problem. But, Alia kept pushing and pushing. He really wanted her to feel it, so finally, he did. And he had to admit—it was really soft to touch!

"What do you think you're doing?"

There was a tiny, squeaky voice behind them both, and when both twins spun around, they were very surprised to see that there was a big hare staring at them both. The hare had very fluffy fur that seemed to be coming off in chunks. And, even stranger, the top part of the hare appeared to be all greys and browns, but the bottom part had great, big chunks of white fur falling out! It looked very odd.

"What are you staring at?" the hare squeaked again, looking annoyed. She did not seem to be happy to be interrupted, and the twins really couldn't blame her. But, they still thought that she looked much different than most of the arctic hares that they had ever heard of.

"Aren't you supposed to be able to hide in the snow?" blurted out Alia, as tactless as ever when it comes to tiptoeing around people's feelings. Arthur elbowed her in the side and shushed her; she was always too loud about her opinions and never stopped to think about what she said, and he hated it!

"Aren't you supposed to stick to your own kind?" snarked back the hare.

Alia shrugged and grinned.

"Well, if you must know," said the hare, puffing herself up and straightening out her back, "I'm losing my winter coat."

"Oh, no! Well, I saw some more of it back there!" Aria pointed back to the last few patches that had been full of the white fluff.

The hare rolled her eyes. "I *know* that. I want to lose it. When I lose my coat in the summer, I can hide better. Can't you see that my back and my nose are both brown right now? That's so I can hide from the foxes in the rocks. I don't want it; I want it gone."

Alia nodded her head. "That makes a lot of sense! It's like changing your clothes for the season! ... Well, almost, except you don't wear clothes!"

Arthur groaned and slapped himself in the face. "Alia, please!" he called out. "Don't embarrass yourself more!"

"What?" Alia replied with a sheepish expression. "I'm just trying to make good, pleasant conversation with this rabbit!"

"*Hare!*" said the hare.

"Hair?" asked Alia.

"Yes!" said the hare.

"Like on your head?" Alia replied, touching her own hair in confusion.

"No! Like *hare! I'm a hare!*" The hare was very clearly beginning to lose her patience with Alia and her lack of understanding, but there was nothing that she could do to make the young human understand.

"Hare! Like H-A-R-E hare." After enough time waiting, Arthur saved her the embarrassment and spelled it out, letter by letter.

"OH! Sorry, Mr. Hare!" Alia replied.

The hare stared at her in shock, like she was debating saying something about how ridiculous Alia was being. "I'm a girl. Clearly."

"Oh, okay! Sorry, Mrs. Hare!" Alia grinned at the hare.

The hare rolled her eyes. That was probably about as close as she'd possibly get, so there was no need to try to force any better understanding. "So, what are you two doing all the way out here? You shouldn't be here at all. There are bears and wolves out here!"

"Yeah, we saw a paw print!" said Alia.

The hare looked frightened. "A big one?" she asked curiously, shrinking down.

"Yep! It was bigger than my hand!" She held out her hand for emphasis and smiled. Alia was not catching on to the fact that the hare did not seem very happy with what was being said. In fact, the hare seemed to be terrified.

"Maybe we should head home, Alia," said Arthur, watching as the hare got more and more nervous.

"Yes, you should!" said the hare. "You don't want to be chased by a bear!" And without another word, the hare took off running as quickly as she could, away from the children.

Alia and Arthur looked at each other. "Let's go, Alia!" said Arthur. "We have to be as safe as we can, and that means not playing outside with bears. Besides, look! The sun is going down! We have to get home!"

So, off the twins went, slowly following the trail of hare fur all the way back to where they started, looking at that little cottage that overlooked the ocean. They entered the door and shut it, slowly taking off their jackets and hats.

With a sigh, Alia looked out the window. "You know, I was really hoping to see something cool today!" But, just then, she saw it! A great, big bear walking right back into the water! It was a polar bear and it was returning from the same path that they had taken. And, it also had two little baby bears with it, too!

And with that, Alia felt much better about her adventure. It may not have been as eventful as she had hoped, but she was thrilled that she had gotten to see the sight of a great, big bear and its babies!

CHAPTER 6: MOUNTAINS OF FUN

Once upon a time, there lived twins that loved each other very much. Their names were Alia, and she was very feisty and very adventurous, and Arthur, who was very proud of himself, but also quite cautious. The twins were practically inseparable! They would do everything together! They were also very special twins, for they shared something that was greater than just sharing a birthday; they shared a very special power with each other! It was a very unique power that helped them greatly, for these twins traveled constantly. They were never put in a school the way most children are; rather, these two children spent their time traveling with their parents and doing their schoolwork on the go!

But, that is not their power. What is their very special power, though, is the ability to speak to animals! These twins were very good at talking to the animals around them. The animals were always a little surprised to hear a human speaking to them, but, they were happy to talk. Some animals would be very kind to the twins; they helped the twins out when they were in trouble. But, other animals did not like the twins much, and they did not like that the twins could talk to them.

No matter where they went, however, the twins knew one thing; they would never be alone so long as they were together and so long as they could continue to speak to animals. After all, animals were everywhere! They were found on the highest peaks of the mountains, and on the desert floor. They knew that, no matter where they went, they could find an animal to talk to; all they would have to do was work hard to find one that would *want* to talk. If they could do that, they could do anything.

One day, Alia and Arthur were brought somewhere new. They were brought to a strange, new mountain range that they had never been to before. It was called the Rocky Mountains, and it went through the United States. Now, the twins were born in the United States, but, they did not spend much time there, as their parents worked very hard as diplomats, going to meet important people in some of the most remote places in the world! But, this time, they were taking a little break. They were there for work, but it was not as busy of work as usual. This time, they were there to meet up with another worker for their company, and that meant that they would get more time than usual with their parents!

This was very exciting for Alia and Arthur, for they loved that very special time with their parents. They loved to be able to walk with them wherever they were going and talk to them without being told, "Hang on; I'm working." And, that very day, they were going to go somewhere very special! They were going to take a hike up the mountain! Alia and Arthur were incredibly happy about this!

So, on the morning of the hike, they all woke up very early, for if you want to be able to complete the whole hike before dark, you have to leave shortly after the sun goes up, and they all got ready to go. Mom packed all sorts of good foods and water. Dad packed lots of sunscreen and bug repellent, and he carried the great, big backpack filled with all of the supplies. Alia and Arthur put on their clothes and their best hiking boots and were ready to go! They could not be more excited to get going than they were right that moment! So, off they ran toward the door, waiting for their parents to follow.

But then, it happened.

The dreaded phone ring. The phone always rang and their parents would always answer it, and then they'd always have to work. Alia and Arthur looked at each other sadly, knowing what was about to happen. They were very used to being told that things were changing and that they would have to try again another time.

But, that time, the phone was ignored and of they went!

"Where are we hiking to?" asked Arthur, standing next to his father. They were all in a cabin near the bottom of the mountain.

"You see that peak? The one that looks a little funny on the top? We are going to that one," replied his father, looking at a map and a compass.

"Woah, all the way to the top?" asked Alia, peering up at the great, big, blue sky with wide eyes. She didn't' think that she'd be able to climb up that high on her own.

"Only if you want to!" answered their mother.

So, off they all went together on their hike. It was the perfect day for one, too; it was late spring, so it was not yet too hot, but also not too cold to go all the way up the mountain. The sun was shining and they could not see a single cloud in the sky. They could hear birds chirping their songs everywhere behind them, sounding as beautiful as ever, and the children were very happy that their parents were finally going along with them on one of their nature adventures! Usually, the adventures were just for Alia and Arthur.

But, on this particular adventure, they had to remember something; they were going to be with their parents, and that meant that they could not make use of their very special power. There was to be no talking to any animals at all.

As they all walked together, Alia stopped to look at something, as she loved to do. There was a patch of the most beautiful white wildflowers growing on the side of the trail! It had purple petals that extended out from the center, and white petals surrounding the calyx within them. The flower was very beautiful and it smelled very nice as well. The smell filled up the air, and it seemed that Alia was not the only one that wanted to stop to smell it. A little bumblebee came buzzing over as well, landing on one of the flowers to suck up some nectar. And, a little further into the patch, Alia could see a hummingbird, dancing through the air. She could hear the soft hum of its tiny wings that flapped faster than any other bird.

Behind her, her mother laughed. "Those are columbine flowers," she said softly. "They are the state flower for Colorado."

"Colorado? Where's that?" Alia asked.

"Here!" answered Arthur. "I think you fell asleep on the plane when we were talking about it. But, we're in the Rocky Mountains in Colorado!

Alia blinked in surprise, but then shrugged her shoulders. "I was tired, okay?" she answered. Then, she heard something— the hummingbird was saying something behind her! It said that it was very tired and very thirsty. But, Alia could not speak back, because her parents were there. A quick glance over at Arthur said that he had heard the little hummingbird, too, and he walked over to stand in front of the flower patch, blocking it out of view just right so that their parents could not see what they were about to do. He reached out his hand for the hummingbird, and whispered, as quietly as he could to the bird to land on his hand.

The bird was very surprised to hear a little boy talking, but happily obliged, and Arthur moved the poor tired hummingbird to a branch to stop to rest without it having to fall to the ground. The bird sung its thank yous to the young children and then settled down for a break. So, off they went to keep on exploring all around the mountains.

They traveled even further away than ever—they were looking for something great and new. So, they kept on hiking along the trial. As they hiked, there were some very pretty birds singing in the trees. Alia could hear some chickadees singing in one, and they could see a blue jay in another. They were very happy to see all of the birds that were in the trees around them, and they all sounded very pretty to listen to. But then, they heard something else. They heard a little voice in the distance, crying out, "Help! Help!"

"Do you hear that?" asked the twins' father.

The children looked at him in surprise. Could he hear the animal, too? So, they all followed their father through the big mountain trail. He was leading them somewhere that was very far away and they left the trail that they had been on, too. They could still hear the crying sounds, and their father still kept on moving forward. Alia and Arthur would look at each other every now and then; they were curious if their father had heard the words too, or if he was only following the sounds of the woods. But, there was no way to know for sure unless they asked.

They went up a slope and then turned and went down another way. They went around some big trees and through some trees that were losing all their leaves. They went over a creek, one by one, splashing in the water, and then, they all stopped! They looked around for what they could find around them, and then they saw it—there was a tiny little raccoon with its head stuck in those little plastic rings that are used to hold together cans at the store when they are bought in packs of six!

The raccoon was stuck on the ground, looking very sad, as it had gotten its head stuck on one end, and the other loops, behind him, were stuck to a branch! It could not get out at all on its own, and it would not be able to do anything at all if they did not help it, and quickly! They were going to have to work very hard to get it untangled from the line, but it seemed like the twins' dad had an idea!

He got very close to the raccoon, who continued ot cry and ask to be left alone. But then, the twins were very surprised to see that the raccoon stopped! It was looking up at their dad in awe! It looked at him and stopped moving, looking down at the ground, even when their dad picked up his pocket knife and sliced up the plastic! He then quickly pushed the plastic into his own pocket so they would be able to dispose of it themselves and stood up.

They heard the little raccoon squeak out a thank you. And, then, something even more magical happened—their father smiled at it and seemed to nod his own head! Could he hear the raccoon too? They stared up at their father in shock as the raccoon ran away, deeper and deeper into the woods on its own.

Their father, noticing the children staring at him, raised an eyebrow. "What is it?" he asked them curiously, watching as the children seemed very unsure of how they should answer their father.

Alia shook her head. She didn't want to ask! The last time that they had tried to tell someone that they could talk to animals, they thought she was crazy.

But, Arthur was braver. "Wow, dad!" he said, very carefully picking out his words. "It was like you were able to talk to that little raccoon to make it stop moving! I've never seen that happen before!" He grinned up at his dad, watching very closely to see if his dad did anything or said anything that would make him doubt that his dad could, in fact, talk to animals just like he could. But, his father did nothing of the sort.

Instead, the twins' father smiled back and patted them on the heads. "You'll understand someday," he said without another word about the subject. "So! It's time for us to finish up our hike, isn't it?"

"Do we have time, dear?" asked their mother, glancing at the sun. It was already more than halfway down; they had spent a lot of their time just looking for the raccoon, and then, helping the raccoon. They weren't upset about it at all, either;

they were very happy that they helped save an animal, but it was kind of disappointing to not get to make it to the top of the peak.

"No, I don't think so," he said sadly. "But, maybe we can call in tomorrow and schedule another hike! One where we don't get so sidetracked by animals that are in need of help!"

The children looked up longingly at their parents. Getting one day with them was already a pretty big treat—but to get two days in a row? That was almost magical and that was something that almost never happened at all! But, if he could make it happen, they would be more than glad to do so!

So, the family hiked back to their cabin together and spent the evening watching their favorite movies, and the next day, they all spent time hiking right back up the mountain. When they made it all the way to the top, they felt like they were on the top of the world! They could see for miles and miles all around them and it was one of the greatest sights that they had ever seen!

CHAPTER 7: TROPICAL TEASERS

Once upon a time, there lived a family of four. There was a mother and a father, who were both very busy with helping people. They loved their work, but oftentimes, it meant that they did not get to spend the time with their children that they wanted. And, there were their twin children. They had a boy and a girl; Alia was the younger twin, but just barely, so the age difference should not count, she always said. And, Arthur was the older twin, and he believed that every second counted, and that meant that he would always be the big bro, and Alia simply had to accept it sooner rather than later! If she could do that, she would have a much easier time dealing with her feelings, after all.

The twins were just like most children their age; they loved to explore the world and play. They loved to spend time with their parents, and they loved to read books all the time. They loved to draw and play games, and they loved to hike and watch movies. But in some ways, they were not like other children their age at all. You see, Alia and Arthur had a very special secret that they did not like to share with anyone. They could speak to animals! No, really; they could speak to animals and have very good, very real conversations with them! They could talk about the weather or about the food that they were eating or about anything else! They could talk about just about anything they wanted to, so long as the animal was willing to do so. And, they were pretty sure that their dad could talk to animals, too, but they were not quite sure.

One day, the whole family had to travel to a tropical island deep in the middle of the ocean. This time, they were on an island that was called Fiji! It was very far in the middle of the ocean, far from just about any other lands. It had beautiful, bright blue water thanks to the fact that it was so far away from everything else, and it had white, sandy beaches that were so big and so soft that they felt like they could live on those beaches and in that sand forever! The twins loved the feeling of the sand under their feet and they felt like it was better than any other sand that they had ever seen before.

Behind them, there were many, many trees growing. The whole land, if you were not looking at the beach, looked like a big blanket of green! It was absolutely gorgeous and as Alia and Arthur walked around on the beach, they felt like they never wanted to leave. "Wow!" said Alia, looking at the beautiful, turquoise water shimmering underneath the sun. There was hardly a wave in sight; it was beautifully calm, and the water was so clear that it was practically transparent!

"You can say that again!" said Arthur as he looked up at a great, big palm tree. Presently, there was a little orange bird sitting in the tree and it was unlike any other bird he had ever seen in his life! It had a strange, green head, but the rest of it was orange. "What a strange looking bird!"

But, the bird looked angry to hear such a thing, and it scoffed and flew away as fast as it could. Arthur felt a little bit sheepish after making the bird angry, but he knew that it would be okay. It would probably just come back later!

Then, he heard another sound—it was a bird that was laughing at them! This bird was bright, lime green and had red little feet and a red throat. "You really messed that one up, kid!" said the bird, laughing and laughing. "Why'd you have to go and make her mad? She's already insufferable enough when she's in a *good* mood and you must made it worse!

The bird looked like he thought it was the most hilarious thing ever, and yet, Arthur felt bad. "I wasn't trying to make her be in a bad mood!" He crossed his arms and stared at the bird.

"Well, you clearly didn't have to! Don't sweat it too much, kid. She's always offended about something. It is better to simply forget it rather than anything else. Enjoy the sun! You don't look like you're from around here anyway; you may as well enjoy your vacation with all of the other humans! Maybe just toss some French fries my way when you get your food or something!" The bird flapped its wings and flew down closer to stare at Arthur. He didn't seem the least bit surprised that the kid had said a word back to him.

"Wait—you knew I could understand you?" asked Arthur, staring at the bird in shock. He had not expected that at all! He was used to other birds and animals being surprised, so when this one wasn't he was the one feeling all of the surprise instead!

"Yup! I could tell! Do you know how?" asked the bird. He flew down closer to Arthur to look him in the eyes.

Arthur shook his head no, his own eyes growing wider and wider. Was he about to learn some great, new secret that could only be revealed to him in the tropics?

"You have the mark!" the bird said.

"The mark?" asked Arthur, surprised. "What mark?" He wasn't sure that the bird was telling the truth, but he would rather learn that he was fooled than possibly miss out on learning the truth because he was not willing to open up his mind to the possibilities of the world.

"You have a mark on your forehead."

"What mark?" asked Arthur, rubbing at his head. The last time he had checked, there was nothing there at all!

"Yeah! You can see it if you take your fingers and make an L shape and then put it on your head!" The bird bobbed his head up and down convincingly as he stared at Arthur. "When you do that, you know!"

So, Arthur did what the bird told him to, but, when he did, the bird only laughed harder and harder at him! It thought it was the funniest thing in the world! "What's so funny?" asked Arthur, rubbing at his head.

"You put an L on your forehead. Loser! Loser!" squawked the bird louder, practically howling with laughter. But, Arthur didn't think that it was funny at all. He felt sad, in fact; he was very disappointed with how things were going.

"Why are you being so mean?" asked Arthur sadly as he looked down at the beach.

But then, over came his father. "What's wrong?" asked Arthur's father with a frown on his face.

"Nothing, dad," said Arthur sadly, looking up at the bird one last time.

"Well," said his father, "Can I tell you a cool little secret?"

Arthur perked up. "What is it?"

"You'll have to come with me to see!" So, Arthur and his father went off, away from the obnoxiously loud little bird and went further and further into the center of the island. "I heard that there is a secret place hidden in these woods!" said Arthur's father.

"Oh, what kind of secret place?" asked Arthur.

"You'll have to see it to believe it! But, believe me, it is the greatest place on earth. I've been there before!" So, off they went together, traveling deeper and deeper. The tropical trees and leaves grew thicker and thicker, and they were longer and longer.

There were birds singing everywhere around them. They were beautiful! They sang songs of magic and songs of adventure. They sang songs of kindness and loyalty. They sang songs of all kind, and Arthur listened very closely to the words as they went. Arthur was quite certain that he could see that his father was listening, too, for his father seemed to turn his head to hear what was going on all around him, just as much as Arthur did. And, that made Arthur smile, for he had had a feeling for a long while that their father could also hear animals the way that he and his sister could. After all, he seemed to know far too much all of the time!

Suddenly, all of the trees disappeared! They were in a clearing, where they could see the great, big tree in the center of the clearing. All above them, they could see the bright, blue sky without a single cloud. It was beautiful! And, underneath the tree, they could see a line up of birds. They were all dancing together! They spun and they swung their wings. They sang and they danced. They jumped and they flipped, and it was the most glorious thing that Arthur had ever seen—and he was seeing it with his father!

But then, something happened. The biggest bird of them all flew down and landed right in front of them. "Ah, Albert!" squawked the bird. "Long time, no see!"

Arthur's father grinned and he held out a hand. "Long time, indeed!" he said to the bird. He looked over at Arthur and winked at him. "You didn't think that you and your sister were the only ones, did you?"

Arthur stared in shock! He had known for a while, but he could not believe it! He was in utter disbelief that his father could also talk to animals! "Does Mom know?" asked Arthur, but his father shook his head. Arthur nodded, looking at the bird thoughtfully. It was probably best that their mother did not know, anyway. She probably would not believe them!

So, from then on, Arthur felt a little bit better about himself. He might have been teased by that bird, but he was not alone! His father could talk to animals just like he and his sister could! His father was just as capable as he was and that was great! So, Arthur smiled at his father and took his hand. "Thanks, Dad," he told him and he felt his father squeeze his hand back.

"I love you, son," said Arthur's father.

"I love you, too!" Arthur replied.

Alia was not the least bit surprised when Arthur told her the truth and all about what they had gone to do that evening. "I told you!!" she cried out. "I! Told! You!" She grinned widely. "Does this mean that we can go on group adventures instead now?"

"You bet it does!" came the sound from behind her, and when Alia turned around, there was their father, waiting for them so they could all go on another hike through the island. "I can't miss out on that great time with you guys, now can I?"

And so, they went on adventures together, and Alia and Arthur felt relieved that it was no longer a secret that they had to keep from everyone else. They were thrilled that they could share with their father, too!

NOW !!!!!! Remember, Mom and Dad, your job is not done.

Reading before bed is one of the greatest ways that you can prepare your child to rest and relax for the day. If you can remember that, you will know that those wonderful journeys that you take your child on before you go to sleep will be the ones that shape and guide their dreams, too. You will help them—you are doing them a favor by reading these stories with your children.

NOW !!!!!! Remember, Mom and Dad, your job is not done.

Reading is something that ought to be encouraged for a lifetime, and while all good things, including books, must come to an end at some point in time, the great thing about books is that you can pick up the next one shortly after! Hopefully, you are able to keep reading with your children and exploring these wondrous new worlds a major part of your life! Hopefully, you are able to remember that these stories can grow with your children—they can help your children learn to explore. They can help your children learn to love reading. They can help your children further develop their own great imagination!

Do not be sad !!!!! From here on out, it is time to read the next stories.

CHAPTER 8: BASIC BEDTIME STORIES: UNICORNS AND OTHER CHARMING CREATURES

The presence of fantastical creatures in children's literature is absolutely ubiquitous: from Aesop's fables to JRR Tolkien's *Lord of the Rings* to modern day tales such as the Harry Potter franchise, the use of magical creatures to appeal to children's sensibilities is everywhere, across cultures and throughout history. The appeal of these creatures is undeniable, and children connect with them for a variety of reasons: primarily, introducing magical creatures expands the possibilities of the storytelling, as their very presence opens the scope of what can happen in a tale. These creatures can provide a source of disruption, creating chaos or righting wrongs, depending on the story, and thus are stand-ins for the young reader herself: when you are young and mostly powerless, it is empowering to identify with the most magical and powerful creatures in a story. These creatures can also help children to act out their most anarchic emotions, such as anger or glee. Think about Max in *Where the Wild Things Are*, where the fantastic creatures allow him to escape the mundane world of bedtime and obedience out into the "wild rumpus" of the imagination.

Unicorns, of course, hold a special place in the hearts of young children: symbolic of innocence and purity, these magical creatures have been mentioned in literature from ancient Mesopotamia to ancient Greece. Essentially, unicorns are horses with a single horn protruding from their head; typically, a unicorn is white in color, and modern depictions often show the unicorn with rainbow colored mane and tail. Original depictions show quite a different— and altogether fiercer—beast, with the enormous feet of an elephant and the bushy tail of a boar. In this way, the unicorn is one of a long list of fantastical creatures that are composites of actual creatures that we know (the griffin, for example, or the harpy). According to some interpretations, the unicorn is mentioned within Biblical text—there is mention of a magnificent horned animal, though some scholars translate the text to mean "aurochs" or wild ox. Still, the unicorn was widely accepted as a symbol of Christ in the early medieval period: as the unicorn was thought to be drawn to young virgins—this is the only way a unicorn can be caught, by being ensnared by a virgin—it came to represent the womb of the Virgin Mary, with the horn as the salvation of humankind (that is, Christ). Cups made of horn—usually rhinoceros horn or the tusk of the narwhal—where immensely popular during medieval times, symbolizing both wealth and piety. You can also find representations and mentions of the unicorn in ancient China and throughout the Islamic world. Thus, it is a magical creature that appeals to many across cultures.

The unicorn is thought to be both fleet-footed and secretive, because its magical nature is compromised so easily, its blood so pure that it can be used to heal other creatures. In legends, the unicorn is often portrayed as prey, hunted down by those with nefarious intentions. This is symbolic of the easily lost quality of innocence: innocence and purity are delicate notions and can be so quickly and irreparably sullied. These very qualities are part of what attract young children to the unicorn, its beauty and strangeness, its sweetness and light. Despite the obviously phallic nature of the horn on the unicorn's head, it is most often associated with the female; again, the idea that innocence is a delicate virtue to be protected (and, alternately, hunted) is most clearly associated with the female, particularly in medieval literature (damsels in distress and such). But the unicorn can also be a strong and fiercely independent presence, as well: as with all magical creatures, the unicorn can be molded to fit into whatever metaphorical lessons you wish to draw.

In contemporary depictions for children, the unicorn is cute and cuddly, with rainbow-colored manes and glittery associations. In contemporary usage for adults, the unicorn has come to mean a rare and valuable asset—like the recent television series, *The Unicorn*, which depicts a single man raising his children and wanting to find romantic and lasting love. The nice, single guy who wants to commit is as rare as a unicorn, the premise suggests. Thus, the unicorn is both, presently speaking, a symbol for non-threatening purity and joy and a symbol for the elusive goodness we all seek. It is no wonder that merchandise and stories about unicorns abound currently. And, perhaps, it is not a bad thing to think that the delicate and pure, the extraordinary and rare can survive in such difficult times. Some modern unicorns can even fly, like the mythical Pegasus, making them even more appealing. While the unicorn has enjoyed popularity throughout the centuries, its hold on popular culture—particularly for little girls, though gender standards are rapidly changing—right now remains as strong as ever. It is one of the most popular of the rotating list of magical creatures that crop up in fantasy stories for all ages.

In general, the most lasting stories, especially for children, are those that combine fascinating imagery and interactive storytelling with morals and lessons that children can learn from. Unicorns and other charming creatures provide the perfect platform for indulging a child's fantasies, granting him or her more agency than is provided in the real world of rules and regulations, and delivering a message of how to act appropriately and with good intentions. They also provide a way in which the author can get the child on his or her side: by rejecting the grown up world of sensible values, and leaving the unimaginative adults behind, children's fantasy literature gives them room to explore their own imaginations and develop their own sense of self. These make for some of the most memorable bedtime stories, the ones that will lead a child into sleep with colorful and happy dreams, frolicking with some of their favorite magical creatures. Read on for some original stories about unicorns and other charming creatures; help your child relax into sleep with some fantastical stories about some imaginary worlds. Their own imaginations and creativity will grow along with them.

CHAPTER 9: AUSTEN'S MYSTERY FOREST

Once upon a time, there was a little girl named Austen who lived in a pretty quiet neighborhood a ways away from a pretty quiet town in a pretty quiet place. She liked school and had a happy home life, but sometimes she was just a little bit bored with all the quietness of her surroundings. But things were just the way they were, and she decided that she would be happy with her quiet life. So, she went to school in the morning, played with her friends at recess, and came home in the afternoon to cuddle with her cat, Silly-Willy, and eat dinner with her family. It was a good life, if sometimes a little bit boring.

Her older sister, Mallory, on the other hand, seemed to have a lot more fun, with all of her older friends doing mysterious things behind closed doors. Austen was only in first grade, while Mallory was in fifth grade, which made her much older and wiser. Mallory would be the first to tell you that she knew a LOT more than Austen, but as much as Austen pressed her to teach her, Mallory refused. "You're just a little kid," she would say. "You'll find out all sorts of stuff soon enough. Until then, just enjoy the simple, quiet things you have." Then she and her friends would giggle and march off to Mallory's room to talk about those mysterious things or ride off on their bikes to have adventures that Austen would know nothing about.

Well, one day, Austen was particularly bored and her adorable Silly-Willy was napping (that was his favorite thing to do, of course), so she decided to go outside and make up a game to play by herself. Austen was a pretty imaginative girl, because she did spend a lot of time playing on her own, so she would make up games about a planet made up only of cats or use the swing set as a space ship. This day, she decided to wander farther away from the house, into the lightly forested area that lay just beyond the boundaries of the neighborhood. Her quiet neighborhood was usually safe, though her mom and dad wouldn't necessarily like it if she wandered too far. "It's just this once," Austen thought. "I just want to see if I can find a really good stick to make into a wand, or a sword."

So, she wandered into the woods behind her house. Well, they really weren't woods, of course, just a clump of spindly trees in an undeveloped lot, but to her, they seemed full of magical potential. She liked pretending that she was in a large forest, hiding from an evil ogre on her way to save the princess. (In her stories, Austen was never the princess, because she thought that would be too boring. Instead, she was the knight, off to defend the princess in her castle. That was a lot cooler, she thought.) This day, she was just looking for the perfect branch, so she wandered amid the trees for quite a while.

She must have started to daydream, because all of a sudden (at least it seemed like all of a sudden), the light seemed to grown dimmer. She knew that she'd be in big trouble if she didn't get back to the house before dusk. It was getting dangerously close to dinner time. Mom would definitely not like it if she weren't back in time for dinner.

So, she started to head out of her pretend forest, having given up on the idea of finding the perfect branch, at least for today, when she heard a soft noise off to her right. It was a light crunching of the fallen leaves followed by a sound that seemed to be a lot like a gentle snort. She froze in her tracks, worried about what scary animal might be lurking in the trees. Her dad had warned her, in his teasing way, that there could be all sorts of dangerous things hidden beyond the boundaries of the back yard. Austen knew, of course, that his warnings were just to keep her safe, and that he was probably exaggerating the stories of wild beasts and abandoned aliens, but her mind flooded with panic at the strange sound beside her. Just as she was about to run as fast as she could, she heard a voice, mild and kind.

"Hello, there, dearie," the voice said, "what are you doing out at this time of day? Everyone knows that magic happens in the hour between daylight and dark."

Austen spun around, less alarmed because the voice was pleasant and friendly but still shocked by the presence of another creature in her pretend forest, and saw a gleaming white horse. Wait, no, it wasn't a horse at all, for it had a great sparkling horn springing from its forehead: it was a unicorn!

Austen didn't think she'd ever been so surprised in all her life. Certainly, most of us would feel that way, stumbling across a unicorn in what was practically her back yard. She didn't quite know what to say.

"Um, excuse me, uh, sir," for she thought that the voice sounded male, "who are you? Where do you come from? How did you get *here*?" The last was perhaps the most important question to Austen, because she simply could not believe that a *unicorn* would be traipsing about in the most ordinary of places.

"I am Gallalahad, young miss, and I come from the Great Magical Forest that connects to all the wooded places on the earth. I can travel from place to place, from forest to forest, just by imagining it in my mind. This little patch of woods became a forest because *you*, my dear, imagined it to be so. The power of the imagination is mighty, indeed. It is our job, as unicorns, to keep the forests both wild and safe. At least as much as we can."

"Safe *and* wild? That seems like those two things don't really match." Austen had a million other questions, but that was the first to pop into her head.

"Yes, little one, it is important that the forests of the world stay wild, with room for animals to roam free and to be wild, like they are supposed to be. If the whole world were like a zoo, with animals in cages, it wouldn't be nearly as much of a magical place, don't you think?" Austen nodded, thinking hard. "And we must also keep the forests safe from too much human meddling, though we are often tasked with making sure special humans are safe as they pass through our forests." His brilliant blue eyes were twinkling.

"Am I one of those special people?" Austen asked, amazed.

"Indeed, you are, young lass! If you hadn't imagined that this rough patch of trees was a forest, than I, Gallalahad, could not travel here. But, since you did, this is actually *your* forest. What shall we call it?"

Austen stood there, her eyes wide and her mouth slightly open, stunned to hear that she had actually invented a whole forest! With magic! And a magnificent unicorn! What could she possibly call it? That was a hard question.

As she was thinking, she noticed that the light was continuing to fade quite fast; if she didn't get moving soon, she would certainly be late for dinner and in big trouble, so she had to put the dazzling creature off for the time being.

"Gallalahad, sir, I thank you for coming here, and I am honored. But I have to get home in time for dinner or else I'll be grounded for a week! Can you please meet me here again, so I can think of just the right name for my forest?" Austen was worried that the unicorn would say no or be upset, but he whinnied softly and nodded his head.

"Certainly, lass, I will be here again . . . as soon as I can," he said as he shook his glittering mane. It looked white when he was standing still, but when he moved his head, his full mane moved about him, glittering with all the colors of the rainbow. It was an awesome effect. "We will meet again, young lady . . . um . . . Miss . . . ?"

"Austen," Austen replied. "My name is Austen."

"Strong name," Gallalahad bobbed his head in approval. "We shall meet again!" And with that, he turned tail—which also glittered with all the colors of the rainbow as he moved—and swiftly disappeared into the further trees.

Austen ran home as fast as she can, just in time to see her sister Mallory setting the table while her mom and dad brought in the platters and bowls of food. She had managed to make it home just in time—though Mallory was a bit put out that she had to set the table all by herself.

The next day—and the next and the next—Austen went out to her forest, the little patch of spindly trees that surprisingly held the sparks of magic, but there was no sign of Gallalahad. She knew that he had plenty of other forests to look after, so it wasn't a surprise when he wasn't there, but it was always a disappointment. She thought that, maybe, she was going at the wrong time of day, and tried to show up as close to dark as she could get away with. But, after many days, there was still no sign of Gallalahad. After a time, she began to think that she dreamed the whole thing up.

Finally, on the verge of giving up, she walked into the forest—*her* forest—not really thinking about the unicorn. She had remembered that she went into the forest that day looking for a branch to make a magic wand with, so she figured that she might as well finish that mission. As she was pulling on lower branches, testing their strength, she heard a slight scuffle and snort and was immediately at attention.

"Gallalahad! You finally came back!" she practically shouted at him.

"Of course I did, Miss Austen, it just always has to be at the right time, when the magic is strong in the air." He beamed at her, shaking his magnificent mane, while his horn gleamed in the fading daylight. "Have you thought any more about what to name your special forest?"

"I have, I really have. I thought and thought and thought and I really couldn't think of anything that was really good." He frowned down at her, looking concerned. "Until," Austen went on, "I thought about what it would mean to any young kid who was bored and lonely, living in a quiet place. To find magic, that's pretty special." The unicorn nodded, an approving look on his face.

"So," Austen went on, "I decided that it shouldn't have a name." Gallalahad looked confused. "I decided it shouldn't have a name, because that would mean that it would be *only* my forest, not a place where anyone could invent their own forest. Making it the No-Name Forest means that it could be anything to anyone who wandered in. It could be whatever kind of magic anyone wanted it to be."

Gallalahad beamed, looking very impressed. "You are a wise and generous young lady, Miss Austen, with considerable gifts to share with others—now and in the future. I accept your proposition and will keep this magical space open for anyone with enough imagination to bring it into being. Good work."

Austen was very pleased that Gallalahad approved, but she was also a little sad. "Now that it's no longer just *my* forest, will I be able to come see you?" she asked, afraid of the answer.

"I'm afraid that I'm not at all sure of that, lass, because magic works in mysterious ways, but . . ." he jumped in as Austen started to tear up, "I can guarantee you that magic follows special people like you always. So, there is always a chance that we will meet again." Austen reached up her arms as Gallalahad bent his neck so she could give him a tight hug.

"Now, run along home, my sweet miss, so you won't be in trouble!" Austen turned to run home, but the unicorn had one more thing to say. "You might consider directing your sister here . . . she might be surprised to find out how interesting her little sister actually is."

Austen beamed at Gallalahad. That would be perfect. Finally, she could show off something she knew that her older sister didn't. Magical times, indeed.

CHAPTER 10: AUSTEN'S AWESOME JOURNEY

Finally, after what seemed like forever, the Fourth of July was here. The grown-ups were setting up grills and makeshift picnic tables, while the kids were running around or biking through the neighborhood or swimming in someone's pool. At around six o'clock, it was time for dinner . . . and a show, though the adults didn't know it yet.

After everyone was done eating their fill, Mallory cleared her throat and announced, as loudly as she could, the premiere of the neighborhood play. "Ladies and Gentleman! Please give us your attention, please! We proudly announce that we have put together a little entertainment for you. With your pleasure, we will now commence our show, 'The Kids of the Kingdom of Keystone Lake Save the Universe!'" With that, she hit the button and music started to play, as Charlie, dressed as an alien, ran into the middle of the gathering and Laken chased him with a fake laser. Austen came galloping in on an old broom dressed up to look like a unicorn, and Matthew played guitar alongside the chaos. There were other kids dressed as alien invaders or as space cowboys and knights and superheroes (Mallory herself dressed up as Wonder Woman, her favorite) fighting them off. None of it really made much sense, but the adults were having almost as good a time as the kids, laughing and shouting in amazement. At the end, Darcy came out, carrying poor Norbert, and pronounced that the Kingdom of Keystone Lake had been saved, as had the universe as a whole. It was truly a triumph of imagination and cooperation that hadn't been seen in many long years.

The next day, Mallory and Norbert received a special award from headquarters and were promised that they would get first choice on any mission they wanted. The fight certainly wasn't over, but they had most definitely made a mark in the struggle to keep imagination alive.

Once upon a time, there was a little girl named Austen, who, you might have heard, lived in a pretty quiet neighborhood a ways away from a pretty quiet town in a pretty quiet place. You might remember that she liked school and had a happy home life, but sometimes she was just a little bit bored with all the quietness of her surroundings. But things were just the way they were, and she decided that she would be happy with her quiet life. Or, at least that was the case until she had encountered a rather gorgeous unicorn named Gallalahad. She happened to be wandering in the wooded area behind her house—it wasn't really a forest until she imagined it was in her mind—at twilight, that magical time of day, and met the very polite and very mysterious beast.

Gallalahad traveled from the central location of the Great Magical Forest to check up on all the forests of the world, making sure they were safe and sound from all the human activity that constantly goes on in the world. It was always a tough job and getting to be tougher, as more and more people lived closer and closer to the forests. He had made a friend in young Austen, because she was smart and kind, and because she had the kind of imagination to dream up a forest and the kind of heart to let it go so others could find it for themselves. No-Name Forest was a special place, an open magical place where anyone could indulge their imaginations. Thus, Gallalahad really liked Austen, because she didn't have a sense of possessiveness or greediness that so many other humans seemed to have. So, he decided, after a time, to revisit Austen at her little No-Name Forest to check in with her and see if she would take up a mission from him and his fellow unicorn caretakers.

After a few days of seeking Austen, Gallalahad began to worry that he wouldn't find her: she was getting older, you see, and she didn't come to her imaginary forest very often any more, as she had other things to occupy her time (all of these electronic thingies, Gallalahad despaired, were preventing children from using their own imaginations!). And Gallalahad couldn't leave the little patch of trees that was the No-Name Forest, for fear of being discovered. He had only to remember the times, long ago, when unicorns tried to wander among the humans. There were too many humans who were interested in using the unicorns for their magic without being very nice about it. So, he just kept visiting the little forest, in hopes that he would eventually see Austen.

Sure enough, on his fifth or sixth visit, he heard her come crashing through the leaves and limbs of these tiny woods—humans were always a little too loud for their own good, he thought—and she jumped in happy surprise when she saw him.

"Oh, Gallalahad! I never thought I'd see you ever again! I am so happy you are here!" With that, she leapt up and gave him a big hug around his neck, kissing him on his cheek. He looked just as beautiful and dazzling as ever, this big white horse with his gleaming white horn and rainbow mane. He was just wonderful, she thought rightly enough.

"Hello to you, as well, Miss Austen." He nuzzled her face with affection. "I am pleased to see you. However . . ." his expression turned grim. "We have some difficult business ahead. I would like for you to travel with me, if you will, to see some things. We unicorns need some special human friends, and I believe that you can be one of them."

Austen's expression also grew grim, as she knew that jolly old Gallalahad would never look so worried if it weren't something terribly important. "Of course, sir, I would do whatever you want me to do, but . . ." she hesitated briefly. "What am I to do about my parents? They'll certainly notice that I'm missing."

"Oh yes, of course," Gallalahad went back to his jovial self, laughing slightly. "We can take care of that easily. We have magic, after all! When we travel, we'll just slow down time a bit here, so that when you get back, it will only be that an hour has passed here, no matter how much time we spend Elsewhere." The way he said Elsewhere thrilled young Austen, eager as always for an adventure.

"Ok, then," she almost yelled, "let's get going." Then, she paused for just a tiny moment. "Um, where is it that we're going? I guess I should ask." She smiled a little awkwardly.

Gallalahad laughed, a sound almost like a whinny. "Yes, yes, of course you should! We are going to check out some of the other forests around the world. I want you to see some . . . things." And again, his face looked sad.

When Austen nodded in agreement, Gallalahad scooped her up with one of his magnificent hooves and placed her on his back—this would be a grave offense if a human were to jump on without permission, as unicorns were very proud animals. You didn't ride a unicorn unless you were a very special friend. With that, he galloped through the thinning trees and into a mist that meant Austen couldn't see anything around her but swirling clouds. It didn't scare her—she was with Gallalahad, after all—but just as she started to get a little concerned, everything cleared up and she found herself in the midst of a forest. A real forest, this time, big and beautiful and filled with the sounds of birds and insects and frogs and monkeys and so many other amazing things that she couldn't yet identify.

"Where *are* we?" she said, in awe. It was hot and damp, and her hair was sticking to her forehead like it had been glued there.

"This, my young lass, is the Rain Forest, the largest forest on earth and perhaps its most important," Gallalahad said grandly. "Many people call this forest the lungs of the planet, because it creates much of the very oxygen that we breathe." Austen looked around her, still amazed; she didn't think she had seen this many living things at once in her entire life. She didn't think there could be anyplace in the world like this.

"This is really cool, Gallalahad! I mean, look at this!" She pointed at a small blue frog resting on a large palm leaf. "That's awesome!"

Gallalahad laughed, "Yes, it is, my dear, but don't touch. That one happens to be poisonous. As is much in this forest." Austen looked alarmed. "But, don't you worry, Miss Austen, you are with me, so you are magically protected from any harm." Austen let out a sigh of relief.

She and Gallalahad wandered around for a bit, taking in all the amazing sights: there were the trees, the tallest she had ever seen, for one; then, there were the monkeys, howling and jumping through the trees, even at the tallest heights; there were what seemed like several dozen species of bright-colored birds, all displaying their brilliant feathers and singing their different songs. There were a million different kinds of insects crawling about—not Austen's favorite thing, but still pretty interesting. She had never seen a caterpillar the size of her dad's hand before. There were also a whole bunch of different frogs, from the size of a fingernail to the size of a small chicken; that was perhaps the most amazing thing to Austen, because she had always liked frogs. She used to collect tadpoles from the pond near her house because she wanted to see them grow into frogs. One year she got into some trouble for putting a bunch of tadpoles in on old glass jar and hiding them in her underwear drawer. Her mom wasn't too happy about finding them. In any case, Austen was dazzled by the sheer amount of plant and animal life on display in this wondrous forest.

"So," she finally broke the silence that had fallen while she and Gallalahad had been looking at everything around them. "Why did you bring me here? I know there has to be a reason, and I'm scared that it's not a good one. You looked upset when you asked me to come with you."

Gallalahad sighed. "Indeed, Miss Austen, not much gets by you. There is a rather sad reason I've brought you here. Of course, I wanted you to see how wonderful this place is, how special it is, how much life there is here. I can see how delighted you are." Austen nodded enthusiastically. "Unfortunately, this place is in grave danger. It is being destroyed each and every day. Let's ride a little further." And he put her up on his back again and, swift as the unicorn's legendary hooves could take them, they were suddenly on the edge of the forest.

"Look, just there," he urged her. Austen saw billows of smoke rising from the ground and lots of men and machines rumbling past.

She gasped. "They're burning it! Why?" It was painful to watch.

Gallalahad snorted. "They're burning it to make more farm land to grow food for animals and people. It's really not their fault. These men are poor and this is their only way to try to help their families. The problem is that this is not the way to help the world or to help themselves. This destruction of the forest will be much, much worse for everyone in the long run."

"What can *I* do about it?" Austen cried. "I'm just one person, and just a kid at that. You know I don't have any power." She looked upset and frustrated.

"But, young lass, that is simply not true," Gallalahad sounded soothing. "In fact, you have all the power in the world. You have a voice and now you have knowledge. This is the only way that things change in the world. People understand and they care, then they speak out and try to help others understand and care. This is why I brought you here, because you will be so important in that effort. You are special, Austen. When you decided not to keep the No-Name Forest to yourself, I knew that you were the right young lady for the job. You understand how important it is for everyone to share, for us to keep some wild places wild so that our imagination and our world stays fresh and new and whole." His eyes gleamed with pride in his young friend.

Austen hugged his neck again. "I guess you're right, Gallalahad. If I know that this is going on, I can try to let others know, and we can work together to find a better way for everyone." She furrowed her brow. "But it won't be easy, will it?"

"No," Gallalahad answered instantly. "It won't. But, you've got a whole lifetime ahead of you to do good work. And I know you absolutely will. But, now, we must get you home." With that, he turned away from the awful sight and whisked Austen away through the mists yet again. Within moments, they were back in the No-Name Forest, with Gallalahad only slightly out of breath. Austen noticed that dusk was falling. She would have to head for home quickly.

"Thank you, Gallalahad, for this journey. I will never forget it." Austen was very serious. "Will I see you again?"

"Ah," Gallalahad looked thoughtful, "I'm not sure, young miss, but you will always remember me. I will be your forever friend and always looking out for you—and the forests of the world. You are growing older and wiser, but you will always have your imagination . . . and your power to do good."

"I love you, Gallalahad," Austen cried. "I *will* see you again, I'm sure of it. Because I'll be back in the forest someday, don't you worry." With that, she turned and ran toward her house, her mind full of knowledge and questions. She was ready to find some more answers, for she did have all the power in the world to know.

CHAPTER 11: SAVING THE KINGDOM OF KEYSTONE LAKE

Thus, Austen would be shocked to learn that her older sister, Mallory, knew lots about magic and even knew a few actual unicorns—though she and Austen's special friend, Gallalahad, had so far never crossed paths. In fact, it was all rather funny that neither sister knew that the other sister had great reserves of imagination for all things magical and wonderful. (It was also true that the sisters weren't the only ones in the family who knew of this secret and boundless magical world; their Gran was also aware of the magical world and would one day tell the sisters about it. But not quite yet.)

One day, when Mallory came home from playing at a friend's house, she saw that Norbert was waiting for her, sitting quite tensely (if a cat can ever look tense, this one was) and knew that something was up.

"Hey, fuzz bud, what' s up?" Mallory had the annoying—to Norbert—habit of speaking in slang terms and calling the old cat just about anything but his name. Norbert, having originally hailed from England, had better manners and more of a sense of what's proper. Perhaps one day he would actually be able to teach Mallory some less American habits. But probably not. After all, he did let her carry him around, draped over her neck, like some kind of fuzzy scarf. It wasn't all that proper, but despite his slight disapproval of some of her habits, Norbert loved Mallory with all his heart.

"Well, darling," Norbert said in his English accent. "It would seem that someone—or some group—has been using magic to keep children from using their imaginations." Mallory frowned, unsure of what exactly Norbert meant. "They are using technology to keep kids inside and stuck in front of screens. With some magical enhancements, these programs and games and shows become so irresistible that kids forget how to make up their own stories and use their own imagination. It's been a problem for a while, but headquarters has asked us to look into it."

Once upon a time, there was a girl named Mallory, who had a younger sister named Austen, and they lived in a pretty quiet neighborhood a ways away from a pretty quiet town in a pretty quiet place. Unlike Austen, Mallory was rarely bored, but it wasn't her group of friends or her many school activities that occupied most of her time, even though her family didn't know it. No, Mallory was rarely bored because she had a companion who was magic and who was with her almost all the time: her beloved cat, Norbert, was actually a member of the Cheshire Guild, which meant that he could disappear and reappear any time he wanted, as well as communicate with his own special companion. That companion, it turned out, was Mallory.

Nobody in Mallory's family had any idea that this grizzled old, fat, grey tabby cat was anything other than a pleasant fixture in the household. Norbert had a habit of lying in front of any closed door to nap, so that anyone coming out of that closed door would inevitably trip over him and stumble or fall. Still, Norbert was friendly and fuzzy so nobody complained about him much. He seemed to sleep, mostly, and to wander about outside when Mallory was at school or over at a friend's house. Nobody knew that this was when Norbert was checking in with magical headquarters to make sure that everything was right in the universe. You see, Mallory and Norbert belonged to a secret organization from which they kept an eye on all the magical comings and goings in the world—it was important to keep up with it, so no one magical creature would get too powerful or decide to do harm. This secret organization had been around since the very beginnings of humanity.

Thus, Austen would be shocked to learn that her older sister, Mallory, knew lots about magic and even knew a few actual unicorns—though she and Austen's special friend, Gallalahad, had so far never crossed paths. In fact, it was all rather funny that neither sister knew that the other sister had great reserves of imagination for all things magical and wonderful. (It was also true that the sisters weren't the only ones in the family who knew of this secret and boundless magical world; their Gran was also aware of the magical world and would one day tell the sisters about it. But not quite yet.)

One day, when Mallory came home from playing at a friend's house, she saw that Norbert was waiting for her, sitting quite tensely (if a cat can ever look tense, this one was) and knew that something was up.

"Hey, fuzz bud, what' s up?" Mallory had the annoying—to Norbert—habit of speaking in slang terms and calling the old cat just about anything but his name. Norbert, having originally hailed from England, had better manners and more of a sense of what's proper. Perhaps one day he would actually be able to teach Mallory some less American habits. But probably not. After all, he did let her carry him around, draped over her neck, like some kind of fuzzy scarf. It wasn't all that proper, but despite his slight disapproval of some of her habits, Norbert loved Mallory with all his heart.

"Well, darling," Norbert said in his English accent. "It would seem that someone—or some group—has been using magic to keep children from using their imaginations." Mallory frowned, unsure of what exactly Norbert meant. "They are using technology to keep kids inside and stuck in front of screens. With some magical enhancements, these programs and games and shows become so irresistible that kids forget how to make up their own stories and use their own imagination. It's been a problem for a while, but headquarters has asked us to look into it."

Mallory sighed. This problem was a bad one and only getting worse. She knew that she had been picked for the mission because she specialized in Technomagicology, the field of blending the science of technology with the art of magic to create new and amazing things. The problem was that this field could be abused, if someone had reason to want bad things—like control over young minds.

"Well, Norbert, I don't think this is a problem we can solve ourselves." Norbert nodded, knowing that a problem this big would take a big effort. "But we can certainly try to help out the kids in our neighborhood. That might create a ripple effect: if we can get these kids to play outside, then they might encourage their friends at school to play outside. And so on. And I think that parents would be happy to see that their kids are doing things other than stare at screens." Mallory thought that there wasn't anything wrong with playing video games or messing with your phone or tablet. It was just that, when it takes up all your free time, it can keep you from using your own mind to think up things and keep you inside too much. Running around outside, especially in the summer, was some of the best fun you can have, Mallory firmly believed.

So, she and Norbert got to work. Mallory began working on a newsletter, while Norbert began an effort to recruit the more intelligent pets in the neighborhood. He was well aware that kids can't resist a passel of puppies or a collection of kittens when it came time to play. Having some animals to lure the kids outside might be crucial to the mission.

Mallory's newsletter, on the other hand, was an attempt to rally the troops (that is, get the neighborhood kids together for a fun event) and create something so fun that nobody could resist. She avoided her computer, much as she loved it, in favor of a hand written newsletter that would have bright colors, different letterings, and lots of doodles on it to get the kids' attention. She had decided to come up with a grand meeting for all the neighborhood kids to decide on putting on a huge show for all the adults in the neighborhood. Everyone would have some input, even the youngest kids like her sister, and Mallory would put it all together. Or, so she hoped.

"Attention All Kids," the newsletter read. "Super-duper Important Meeting To Be Held at the Dinosaur Fort at High

Noon on the 18th of June. Be There or Be Square. Bring Snacks and Pets." The Dinosaur Fort is what the neighborhood kids called the small ravine in the center of the neighborhood; it was filled with a bunch of old shale rocks that everyone was convinced held the fossilized remains of unknown dinosaurs, though so far, nobody had actually found anything. Over the years, bits of wood and old tin had been scattered around and arranged to provide seating and a rough version of shelter. It was just a good central place for everyone to meet.

Mallory rode around the neighborhood on her bright red bike, putting a copy of the newsletter in every mailbox. While this was perhaps officially frowned upon, the neighborhood adults put up with Mallory's occasional newsletters. Mostly they smiled and shook their heads, wondering what that girl was up to now.

On the day of the meeting, just about everyone showed up, about nineteen kids in all, with Paul out due to a broken arm and Becky gone off to camp. Mallory explained her plan.

"So, we are going to put on a show for the Fourth of July, before the fireworks." The neighborhood was small and remote enough that all the families gathered together to shoot off fireworks at the holiday every year, with various grills going with hot dogs and hamburgers galore. "This will show all the adults how smart we are and how grown up we are, that we can do this thing on our own." Mallory knew that the best way to get kids to organize was to convince them that no adults were necessary. "We need ideas from everyone, so I can put something together. Then, we'll come back next week and assign parts to everyone and make a rehearsal schedule."

Not all of the kids were super excited about the project, but once Mallory let them do whatever they wanted—some kids didn't want to perform, but they were happy to make costumes and props, while other kids were more interested in being lone action heroes rather than be a part of the group—pretty much everybody was on board. Mostly, everyone wanted to show the adults how awesome they were and the idea that this would be a total surprise was also a lot of fun.

The next week, Mallory gathered up everyone's ideas (and there were many) and put to work constructing a kind of show around them. Austen, of course, put forth the idea that a magical unicorn lived among them, while one of her good friends, Matthew, wanted to be able to play his guitar. Laken wanted to have a laser and fight aliens, while Darcy (who was almost as bossy as Mallory) insisted that she get to play a queen of some sort. Mallory wasn't sure how she was going to fit it all together, but really, it didn't much matter: she had succeeded in getting everyone's imagination going wild. She had even convinced Norbert to allow her to dress him up like a little prince for Darcy to hold.

In the weeks leading up to the Fourth, everyone would hang out around the Dinosaur Fort, practicing this and that, mostly goofing around, with Mallory barely trying to contain the chaos. It was going to turn out to be the best summer of her life, thus far, she thought. All these kids, learning to work together and using their imagination to make something . . . well, if not great, then certainly interesting: it was exactly what headquarters wanted.

Finally, after what seemed like forever, the Fourth of July was here. The grown-ups were setting up grills and makeshift picnic tables, while the kids were running around or biking through the neighborhood or swimming in someone's pool. At around six o'clock, it was time for dinner . . . and a show, though the adults didn't know it yet.

After everyone was done eating their fill, Mallory cleared her throat and announced, as loudly as she could, the premiere of the neighborhood play. "Ladies and Gentleman! Please give us your attention, please! We proudly announce that we have put together a little entertainment for you. With your pleasure, we will now commence our show, 'The Kids of the

Kingdom of Keystone Lake Save the Universe!'" With that, she hit the button and music started to play, as Charlie, dressed as an alien, ran into the middle of the gathering and Laken chased him with a fake laser. Austen came galloping in on an old broom dressed up to look like a unicorn, and Matthew played guitar alongside the chaos. There were other kids dressed as alien invaders or as space cowboys and knights and superheroes (Mallory herself dressed up as Wonder Woman, her favorite) fighting them off. None of it really made much sense, but the adults were having almost as good a time as the kids, laughing and shouting in amazement. At the end, Darcy came out, carrying poor Norbert, and pronounced that the Kingdom of Keystone Lake had been saved, as had the universe as a whole. It was truly a triumph of imagination and cooperation that hadn't been seen in many long years.

The next day, Mallory and Norbert received a special award from headquarters and were promised that they would get first choice on any mission they wanted. The fight certainly wasn't over, but they had most definitely made a mark in the struggle to keep imagination alive.

CONCLUSION

For many children, getting to sleep can be a fraught process, and the technique of employing bedtime stories to help lull them into rest is also a nearly timeless one. Additionally, fostering mindfulness and understanding meditative practices can be a part of this process, soothing children into sleep and fostering a calm and peaceful mindset for their daily lives. Storytelling can create a world of visualization that helps children develop coping skills for external events over which they have no control; this creates a state of mind that eases into relaxation and rest.

The power of bedtime stories for both adults and children cannot be overstated. Not only do they provide some of the best quality and bonding time between parents and children, but they also unlock the power of imagination, visualization, and mindfulness. This kind of power leads to healthy psychological development and sound physical routines, such as routine bedtimes. By combining the power of storytelling with the practices of mindfulness and guided meditations, you are also fostering a child's ability to be calm, relaxed, and grateful in their everyday lives. This kind of well-being and happiness are truly priceless.

If you have enjoyed these tips, techniques, and various tales, don't forget to explore the other fantastic realms of bedtime stories in the entire series: Bedtime Stories for Kids, Books 1 through 2. Book 2 contains original lullabies and re-tellings of classic stories, faeries, fantasies, adventure stories, stories that focus on the wider world and the magic of nature. You will find yourself immersed in a world of wonderful stories and boundless imagination, all while spending valuable time with your child and helping him or her off to sleep.

CPSIA information can be obtained
at www.ICGtesting.com
Printed in the USA
BVHW050315080521
606757BV00009B/1228